THE SCHOOL NURSE FROM THE BLACK LAGOON

STORY BY
MIKE THALER

PICTURES BY
JARED LEE

Cartwheel
·B·O·O·K·S·®

SCHOLASTIC INC.

New York   Toronto   London   Auckland   Sydney
Mexico City   New Delhi   Hong Kong   Buenos Aires

In Loving Memory of Romeo Muller — M.T.

To All the Dear Nurses, Who Are Always There — J.L.

Visit us at www.abdopublishing.com Reinforced library bound edition published in 2011 by Spotlight, a division of ABDO Publishing Group, 8000 West 78th Street, Edina, Minnesota 55439. This edition was reprinted by permission of Scholastic Inc. No part of this publication may be reprinted in whole or in part, or in any form or by any means, electronic or mechanical, without written permission of the publisher. For information regarding permission, write to Scholastic Inc., Attention: Permissions Department, 557 Broadway, New York, NY 10012.

Printed in the United States of America, Melrose Park, Illinois.
082010
012011

Library of Congress Cataloging-in-Publication Data
This title was previously cataloged with the following information:
Thaler, Mike, 1936-,
 The school nurse from the black lagoon / by Mike Thaler ; pictures by Jared Lee.
    p. cm.
 [1. Nurses--Fiction. 2. Schools--Fiction.] I. Lee, Jared D., ill. II. Title.
 PZ7.T3 Se 1995
 [E]--dc20   98103618

ISBN: 978-1-59961-798-5 (reinforced library bound edition)

All Spotlight books have reinforced library binding and are
manufactured in the United States of America.

There's supposed to be a nurse at school.

No one's ever seen her.

At least, *no one that's ever come back.*

They say her office is behind the principal's.

Her name is MISS HEARSE THE NURSE
and she's supposed to be a *REAL* GHOUL.

All around her office are supposed to be dripping color pictures
and see-through statues of body parts:
eyeballs on rubber bands, heads filled with brains,
and bodies stuffed with everything else!

She's also supposed to have a skeleton hanging in the corner.
They say it's a kid who went there with a stomachache.
She *cured* it!

She never leaves her office.
She must eat her lunch there.

They say she is always ready for *any* emergency.
Once a kid got cut in half using the paper cutter.

They say Miss Hearse gave him a Band-Aid and sent him home.

Another kid got run over by the media cart
and was flattened.
He's now the rug in her office.

You don't go there unless you're *really* sick!
And she knows if you're faking.
She has a thermometer the size of a flagpole.
It can read the temperature in your toenails.

She has tongue depressors as big as surfboards,
so you should only go there with *major afflictions*.

Then there are the "TESTS."
She measures your height against a wall chart.
If you're too short, she stretches you on the "RACK"
until you reach the line.

Then you have the eye chart.
If you can't see the BIG "E,"

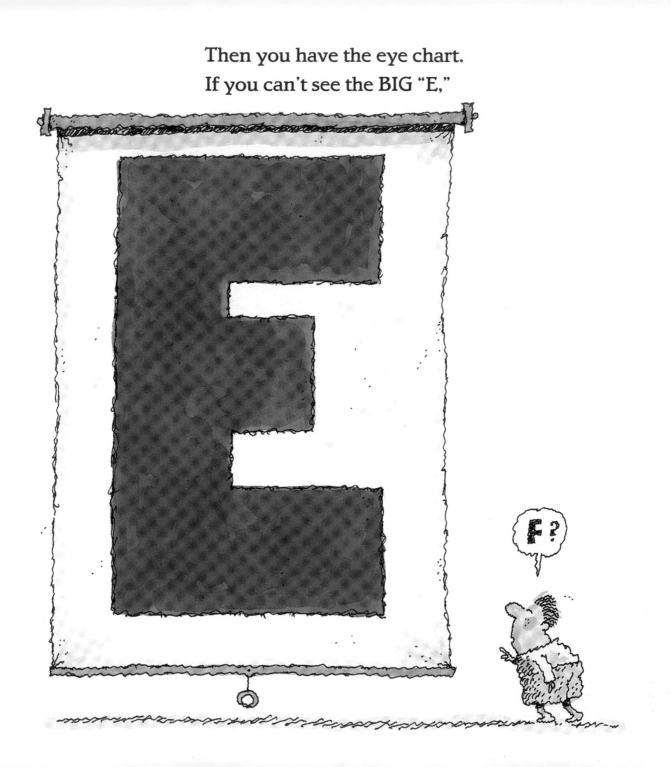

she uses your eyeballs for billiard balls.

After that, there's the "HEARING TEST."

If you don't pass, she puts your ears in her jewelry collection.

Next there's the "VACCINATION."
Her needle is so long, she can vaccinate six kids at once!
It's sort of like shish kebab.

And there's always the "ICE."
If you fall down, she puts you in her "FREEZER."
Some kids take *all* summer to thaw out.

There's also the "COT."
The mattress is filled with bricks
and the pillow is filled with rocks.
The blanket is made out of sandpaper.

On the first day of school,
Penny Weber went there for a nap.
She hasn't straightened out since.

Eric Porter went there with a toothache.

Now we call him "GUMS."

Freddy Jones went there with a sore throat.

Now his head is attached *directly* to his shoulders.

Oh-oh, I'm breaking out in blue dots.
They are all over my hand.

I must have *leprosy*!
My hand will fall off.
I'd better go to the school nurse.

I walk into her office.

Freddy Jones is taking a nap.

Either that, or he's dead.

Miss Hearse is sitting at her desk. She looks pretty normal.

I show her my hand.
She wets a paper towel and gently rubs.
The blue dots disappear.

She asks to see my pen.
I take it out of my pocket.
She shows me where it's leaking.
She smiles and gives me a new one.

She's a miracle worker.
I'm cured!

She pats me on the head,
and tells me to visit anytime.

I go back to class and write her a thank-you letter...

with my *new* pen.